PROMISE OF HUMANITY

Marcial Villarroel S.

Title: Promise of humanity
Author: Marcial Villarroel S.
Translation: Shiara Mel
Layout: Rafael Berdeja
Cover design: Carlos Egüés
Cover image: Matthewa Fflecat virus

As a form of solidarity aid in this Coronavirus pandemic, 100% of the author's royalties on this book will be donated to people without food in Bolivia.

his book was originally written in the Spanish language. If you have any doubts about the translation, consult the original version in Spanish.

FOREWORD

Promise of humanity, is a narrative framed in fantastic reality, from a futuristic vision, about events after a deadly pandemic that occurred in the 21st century.

Without losing the human and emotional nuance that characterizes the daily life of people at any time or time.

Where despite the cold and distant social norm that governs behavior in a reconstructed new technological and advanced order, the way is opened and the evolution of emotions and feelings prevails, which all believed to have been lost.

MARCIAL VILLARROEL SILES

Bolivian, studied Economics and a Master in Banking & Finance. He has written and published since he was twenty years old. He lives in Santa Cruz de la Sierra, Bolivia.

CONTENT

PROMISE OF HUMANITY

NARRATIONS

CHAPTER ONE

A peaceful and calm life

Staring at the wide holographic screen in front of her face, standing and absentmindedly reviewing the scores in the academic reports. Ilana hadn't even noticed she was being watched by someone else named Evans. That while still standing at the door of that great room dedicated to the investigation of binary molecules, he had decided to stay there a moment longer to observe her with a certain disguise.

Because being classmates in that course in environmental genetics, he had not been able to hide his excessive interest, by turning his eyes every moment during the progress of the class and towards her.

Despite not having been warned by most of the other students on campus, the same did not happen with Spencer, Evans' roommate. Nor with Aurora, Ilana's research partner, who did not live with her in the same home, although they were assigned to live together from the day of their births.

As was the customary norm in the entire known world, and since memory was had.

Because existing all the human beings without direct relatives, each one of the six hundred million people that existed in the world, were assigned to live in pairs. Not for reasons of a sexual nature or for affective considerations, but more than anything for social reasons and living together.

Peacefully coexisting the entire world population, during the last three centuries, in those six urban mega-colonies, concentrated equally in the gigantic staggered towers of two hundred floors or levels. That they were the only buildings erected and located in each of those half a dozen landmasses, where the towers had been rebuilt after the great catastrophe.

In that each urban mega tower housed a hundred million people, distributed from half a million beings in the intra-technological cities, existing by each level or floor of the gigantic stepped towers. Whose autonomous and mechanical operation made them independent of human intervention, as they had been programmed since its construction several centuries ago.

Where, despite the fact that nobody had the impulse to break any of the rules that governed social harmony, which was lived in each of those six urban mega-colonies.

Nor was the presence of the automated security and surveillance drones, which with their spherical shape of half a meter in diameter, safeguarded that peace not be broken with their continuous rounds through all levels and corridors, which they did daily in each of the staggered towers.

Because with countless lenses, like spy eyes, in all their metallic surroundings, nothing seemed to escape the vigilant scrutiny of those silver and spherical probes.

Created more than three centuries ago and flying ever since in groups of three, both in the bright light of day and in the dark shadows of night.

Without anyone being able to limit that automatic and intimidating surveillance, which was only controlled by the central data matrix. That he also supervised all the life supports in each of those six enormous towers of two hundred floors, which each housed a hundred million inhabitants.

Capitol city being the first colony that had been put into operation, where Ilana and Evans had lived for three hundred years. Dedicating themselves, like most citizens, to scientific research, to improve life in all its forms, both in the flora and in the fauna that surrounded them.

Although they were not exempt from enjoying the sonic pleasures of music or from analyzing historical records through the data network, for the satisfaction of incurring in research or only some type of personal and intimate entertainment.

As Ilana and Aurora did, they did not miss the Symphonic Studies Musical Unit every afternoon, where the two participated, playing Ilana a sweet flute, with Aurora doomed to play the piano.

That it had become a routine for both of them during the last couple of decades, seeking the perfection of each sound emitted, as was the programmed norm in everything that was done on a daily basis.

Although neither did they fail to observe the two, as part of their biological investigations, the behavior of the various animals that had repopulated the reforested land in ancient times.

After having been many species saved from the almost total disappearance, or even revived from the evident extinction, with the partial or total organic reconstruction of those new or old species, from some sample of living tissue or cell.

That made it possible to observe in the extensive and wooded groves, swamps or plains that surrounded each of the gigantic stepped towers. Those singular animal silhouettes that, walking alone or in flocks, were not only of mammals or birds of the modern era, but also of those diverse herbivorous creatures of the Jurassic and Cretaceous period.

Because it was not strange to see from the windows or from the various observatories placed on each floor, those innumerable dinosaurs of the strangest sizes and colors, who fearlessly wandered through the skies or among the vegetation of the trees and bushes at ground level.

That it drew considerable attention especially to Ilana, when comparing the behaviors and behaviors, which were considered primitive or wild in all the studies or investigations of the time. But especially in the monkeys that were the most similar to humans.

- Why are you so obsessed with investigating these primates? - Was the question that Aurora sometimes asked her fellow student.

When contemplating together on some holographic screen of the pavilion of zoological studies, that recurrence of synaptic patterns in the head of a whole herd of apes.

That they could observe through a biological microcapsule inserted into the cerebral cortex of those animals, while they played or wandered in the wooded region and outside the huge tower.

That in addition to a merely scientific interest, Ilana also aroused another sense of curiosity about aspects of social relationship, showing the emotional ties between each of the members of that family that was considered wild and primitive.

Where the sense of protection between a mother and her offspring was outstanding, such as the anger and violent rivalry between two males who competed for the affection of some female from the same herd.

That, although Ilana understood, how those behaviors were the result of chemical variation in the hormonal gland. Despite the years of observation and study, she could not understand the affective or sentimental essence, which was involved in the emotional bond that arose in the coexistence of those furry animals.

- It is not unnecessary obsession! - Ilana sometimes answered, without turning her eyes and with a certain coldness in each of her words - I just don't understand why there is that crucial difference of emotions and feelings, between humanity and these apes, if we have almost ninety-nine! eight percent in similar chromosome patterns!

- I'd tell you it's evolution! - Aurora said to her, one of those times - But I know it would not be enough before all your concerns.

- It's because you have known me for several centuries! - Ilana replied, not daring to smile, so as not to be discovered with a different attitude.

She prefers to continue pretending the coldness of always in her face, being in public and in front of other people.

Because even though Aurora was her assigned study partner, Ilana knew that she and, as happened with most of the other people, would not hesitate to report her to the Data Center, given the irregularity of seeing her smile or with some feeling alien to the interest in healthy and pure research.

So while Ilana had not been indifferent to Evans' sneaky stare, she also didn't dare give back any interest in the boy. Despite the fact that she also could not avoid a certain impulse to smile when seeing him or being at a close distance between them.

In the same way that seemed to happen to Evans, who also did not hide his distrust and suspicion of Spencer, his roommate. And before whom it was difficult to change the rigidity and seriousness in his countenance, only to dare to look away from Ilana, when that companion was not near or at his side.

- You know that sometimes I don't understand the distortion of your behavior! - Aurora sometimes said to Ilana, without turning around, keeping her face bent over an electron microscope. That he was safe observing some sample of biotic tissue.

- What do you mean? - was what Ilana murmured, with a certain indifference in the words, as she was also doing the same, with another sample of vegetable sap under the lens of her own microscope.

Since both of them did not talk much, nor were they distracted from carrying out their respective biological investigations, more than once Ilana had been surprised by Aurora.

Who had accidentally noticed how she approached with feigned concealment towards Evans. That he also didn't bother much to pretend when he met Ilana's gaze.

That it became a curious fact before the logical and frequent reasoning of Aurora, as also happened to a lesser degree with Spencer. When the two watched without understanding, as Ilana and Evans did not respect the social distance of one meter allowed.

Noticing even sometimes how Evans dared to touch one of Ilana's thin, smooth hands with his fingers.

Waking up in Spencer, some of those mornings, the interest to ask, why his partner had done that, referring to the contact of hands.

- The truth, I did not realize! - It had been the evasive answer, that Evans gave him most of those repeated occasions.

Not forgetting Evans either, be more careful next time, being close to your stiff housemate.

That was one of the reasons for Ilana and Evans to redirect several of their research work on genetic biology, to agree on the immediate results.

And so, with that excuse and in that way, they will be reassigned to work together in some subsequent stages of the study process.

Without anyone and especially Aurora or Spencer, they could suspect that something unusual was being born in those two hearts, when Evans and Ilana met eyes, even for a brief moment.

And despite the fact that the programmed lack of emotions and feelings, which limited their attachment, was not the greatest obstacle to a more intimate affective relationship.

Neither was unaware that it was more than anything that they lacked internal reproductive biological organs in women, preventing any one of them from thinking of some kind of human sexual reproduction in the old-fashioned way.

Because, although Ilana had been procreated in one of the innumerable amniotic chambers three hundred years ago, as was the characteristic in all that new generation called "primary", with perfect health and absence of aging.

Although she maintained the female gender in most of her physical appearance, which she had inherited from her genetic predecessor. Nor did she consider herself totally a feminine creature, not feeling the hormonal changes that women once had to have experienced with the ability to reproduce and develop life in their maternal bellies.

While for his part, Evans, with those same and improved health characteristics, which were not far from immortality due to indefinite longevity, had also been procreated three centuries ago, and maintained the physical appearance of the male gender by his genetic predecessor.

For this reason, although the coexistence between all human beings was not legally prohibited, there were no known cases of affective unions between these two genders.

With quite evident differences under the white clothes that covered their rather tall and thin bodies.

That both Evans and Ilana had it very much in mind, the many times they spoke or when crossing their eyes when they were face to face.

Although neither of them could not avoid thinking of each other, such as even dreaming of each other that they walked hand in hand or walked under the countless trees, which were in the ecological external park on the outskirts of the immense urban tower.

That it would have been the only thing in that reiterated attitude of looking at each other from a distance, that they had during the last ten years since they met, if it had not been for Evans, who was encouraged more one afternoon when they walked almost alone through a wide and long corridor of the intra city where they lived.

- I wanted you to know! - Evans said - That there is something strange that I feel in my chest when I see you! - I hesitate for a moment to continue saying - And I can't imagine being able to live if I'm not by your side! - He added later, with the conviction that was characteristic of him, when he expounded a theory or some postulate of genetic biology.

That he said, without taking his gaze from her eyes either, when absentmindedly and almost accidentally, he also reached out to take Ilana's hand and place a delicate cobalt ring on one of her delicate fingers.

- What does this mean? - she asked, with an unusual tone of innocence in her voice, next to the funny gesture of surprise in her eyes.

- It means I want to be with you, more than with someone else! - Evans replied, with a slight smile on his face, but not of victory but more like a gesture of supplication and approval of his recent words.

- You know I feel the same about you too! - Ilana exclaimed in a soft voice, knowing within herself that this was the right answer.

While placing her hand and that ring on her finger, in front of her eyes, she also did not avoid smiling with innocent mischief.

When he kissed her on the cheek, which for both of them was the first that had been given and received in all that time they knew each other.

Although after that short and emotional moment, with the promise of saying nothing or revealing that mutual secret, the two of them only said goodbye with a slight shake of the head, and with an ill-concealed, otherwise evident and notorious.

Then they both walked in opposite directions, with Evans heading towards his home, which he shared with his partner Spencer. While she walked to the medical center, where that morning she would meet her father, who would have one of his clinical checkups every fifty years, while waiting for a new and routine organ transplant.

CHAPTER TWO

Feelings of strange emotion

Another of those afternoons and just a few moments after lunchtime, Ilana, who always wore an impeccable white suit, loose-fitting pants, with a collarless jacket and long sleeves, as was customary with all medical researchers, also arrived smiling to the apartment he shared with his father.

After traveling for a few minutes on the vertical public transport, which went up and down between the two hundred levels of the huge and erect stepped tower. That housed that urban mega colony of a hundred million people.

Where she had descended, from biotic research laboratories at level one hundred and eighty-three, to her home on the one hundred and twenty-sixth floor. That being one of the two hundred intra cities, it had domestic neighborhood characteristics, with its half a million citizens in all that inhabited level.

Where it was something more than peculiar, that irregular situation of Ilana with her father, as she was the only person in all that urban colony, as in the entire known world, to have a pseudo-parent of the old seed generation and also with an aging body still alive.

If Reymond Cox could receive that title of paternal kinship, for having been the one guiding her with paternal affection, as soon as Ilana had been procreated in one of the amniotic cloning chambers, which had been in each urban colony for more than three centuries.

- How was your class this morning? - Reymond asked him, with an absent-minded attitude, while sitting and looking at a small open book that he was holding in one of his hands.

- It was a regular and calm morning! - She replied, still bringing her face closer to his, to kiss him on the forehead, as they both used to do only in the privacy of their home, at that time when families no longer existed or physical approach was not allowed Between people.

- I notice you livelier than other days! - added Reymond, with a smile - Although I do not understand why you continue attending those courses in biology and classical history, if you are already an expert in both subjects, and more in history with my stories!

- But listen to your somewhat uncertain stories! - Ilana replied with a smile - they do not count as academic credits! - He added later, with a gesture of joy on his face - Although I am the one who does not understand, how can you still like to read these paper copies, when you have the virtual links that would allow you to download all the books you want directly in your head!

- It's because of the romantic mystery of reading! - Reymond said, as he placed the book on a small table next to him and next to the chair in which he was sitting. Where he also placed the classic rimmed glasses, he was wearing.

Without avoiding either of them, smiling again after crossing their eyes, at her invitation, to sit together at the circular table in the small dining room.

To savor the food that Ilana had chosen from the food dispenser, as she used to do every day when she returned to their home.

Although unlike the same routine that they had been repeating for the last couple of centuries, this time, Ilana remained somewhat silent as she brought the first bites to her lips.

- What's going on? - Was Reymond's question, without imagining the effusive answer he would hear from his daughter.

- I think I'm in love! - She replied smiling, placing the fork on top of her almost empty plate.

- In love? - He murmured, with some doubt in his eyes - But how would you know, if that emotion does not exist these days? - He finally concluded, with a sincere shine of paternal love in his eyes, when he observed his daughter.

- Because of the stories, about how you met my mother, when they were just young. Plus, the way you always talk about her in your stories! - Ilana replied.

Knowing in her heart and especially in her mind, that those definitions she had used were not consistent with the obvious reality. Since all the people who lived, with the exception of Reymond only, were true clones and there was none born from a mother. Although Ilana also could not deny the version of the one that Dad called with affection, and that she had ever verified it in the original records of the blood samples, which were available in the database of the computer system.

Where it was indicated that she carried the last name Cox, because Reymond's daughter had been her genetic predecessor.

Because Ilana being the clone of his daughter, as specified in the stored records. She must have had a mother, as he had told her many times, from the first times that Ilana had heard him somewhat incredulous and lying in bed. As Reymond told her stories before carefully tucking her in.

- So, you know what love is? - Was the soft and expectant question of that father. With the intention of getting her daughter's attention back, visibly distracted by her mental musings.

- Of course not! - She replied, with an air of greater wisdom in her eyes, as she also contemplated him with a remarkable glow of affection - Because with all the information she downloaded on the subject and even with the emotional way you have, when you tell me your romantic anecdotes With my mother, I don't really know how to define love as emotions!

Getting Ilana that Reymond smiles after hearing those words, to extend both arms seeking to reach her hands.

- It's true dad! - Ilana murmured, with a certain reluctance in her voice and after lowering her gaze. At the same time, he felt the warm touch of his father's fingers on both hands.

- The first thing I felt when I knew I was about to fall in love! - He said, with the clear intention of reviving her - It was that fast heartbeat that sometimes made me forget everything bad when I was around your mother!

- It was for phenylethylamine! - She said, without containing a slight smile on her lips, seeing the expression of tender scolding that he showed her in his old eyes.

- You know I wasn't just talking about that! - added his father, looking up for a moment at the ceiling.

- I know dad! - Ilana replied - But there is nothing you tell me now that I would not have heard or read.

- Then there is only one thing left to do! - Reymond said, with a smile of affection and mischief, as he looked tenderly at his daughter again.

- What do you mean? She murmured, returning the same kind of joy on her face.

- That you will know everything when you give your first kiss on the lips! - He replied, looking at her in silence for a moment.

That, despite being an irrational comment, that no one else would have said, for being outside the protocol of reflective behavior and above all alien to any type of emotional control. Nor did it disturb her, who kept her expression cold and expressionless for a moment, before fixing her gaze on her father's warm, smiling face.

- What an absurd idea! - Ilana exclaimed, with the childish expression of a certain revulsion and disgust - On the lips it is otherwise unhealthy and not hygienic! - He added then, shaking his head to the sides, before standing up and with both empty plates in his hands, to go to place them in that automatic dishwasher that was in the kitchen.

But despite the fact that she preferred not to mention that topic for a time, avoiding any comment by Reymond about it. Knowing the liberal and rebellious inclinations towards strict rules, which his father obviously did not obey.

Nor could he remove from his mind that unusual suggestion, which, although it had not been practiced in more than three centuries, did not seem so irrational and impossible, every time he thought about it or imagined the ways in which she could do it.

Without avoiding after several months, to cheer up to make the same suggestive comment to Evans, his best friend so to speak. When they both walked conversing menacingly under the trees in the outer park that bordered the gigantic tower in which they lived.

- A kiss! On the lips! - Evans exclaimed, with the same expression on his face, just as Ilana had had several months ago, when he heard that suggestive idea from his father's mouth.

- What's wrong with it? She asked, with a pretense of calm and innocence. To hide the shame that she really felt inside and that did not avoid reddening her cheeks, at the unusual suggestion that she herself could not believe she had made.

Achieving Ilana that his friend Evans, also infected by curiosity, could not have removed that new and peculiar idea from the head.

That little by little penetrated more into his male mind, until he reopened memory files and memories that had been inactive, since he opened his eyes when he came into the world three centuries ago.

- What is happening to me? - Evans was questioning himself, analyzing his distorted health indicators, which were projected in his mind under the biosecurity and medical control chip that he had in his body, like any other citizen in the world.

That he did it repeatedly, after each strong throbbing in his chest, when he saw Ilana, even if it was at a distance or not so close to her.

In the same way, which also seemed to happen to her, who, feeling an inevitable joy when approaching him, not only smiled excitedly, but looked for any excuse to also bring her fingers close and almost accidentally touch one of Evans' hands.

That it became a routine and quite hidden game between the two. That, although it was not expressly prohibited under any legal norm, nobody used to do it or get so close, always keeping for a habit and for almost three hundred years, the prudent distance of one meter between each individual.

Still, imagining or indulging in any kind of physical contact, which had been the general norm for those three centuries. Since each of the people had been created from their genetic predecessors, and through the cloning of new perfect and long-lived bodies.

In those countless amniotic chambers that had controlled rebirths within the six urban colonies scattered around the world.

That was not an impediment for Evans and Ilana to see that strange feeling grows in their hearts, during each of those new days that began to pass together.

Without holding back one morning, after seeing each other for a whole year and almost daily, to encourage each other to bring their mouths closer and barely touch their lips, in an almost childish kiss.

When the two of them had their faces down and side by side, above a small electron microscope.

- This is more than phenylethylamine! - They both thought almost at the same time, sharing their thoughts under a mental and electronic link, as it was customary to stay in the study laboratories, after separating their faces to look at each other smiling and staring for a slight and short moment.

- This is Love? -Was the question Evans muttered.

- If it is! - she whispered - It would mean that we are in love?

The two of them smile again with that unusual conclusion, as they later continue walking with disguise and without showing any emotion in their gestures or words. While removing the white coats to disinfect in the alpha radiation chambers, before the entrance or exit door. As it was always done before leaving that laboratory of practices and study on medical biosecurity.

- Do you think they reprimand or perhaps call our attention? - It was Evans' question, when he noticed about three traveling drones passing over their heads, as he walked next to her and among the other people. That they still walked through the wide corridors, without approaching even less than a meter away from each individual.

- We weren't breaking any rules! - Ilana replied, with a disguised smile and without turning her face, as she continued walking very erect and with her eyes fixed on a distant point on the horizon.

Although later, with their slim and spiky silhouettes, in which almost everyone was over two meters tall, only Evans and Ilana were the only ones who from time to time turned their eyes slightly between them, to exchange a wink or a brief smile on his lips, walking silently among that swarm of passers-by impeccably dressed in white.

CHAPTER THREE

Awaken heart

Although the civilized world had changed in the last three centuries, the old and vast cities disappeared along the horizon. All of them were transformed into reforested or cultivated fields, to give way to the planned construction of unique and enormous staggered towers of more than two hundred floors.

Scattered one by one, in the six continental regions throughout the world, and that concentrated a genetically renewed population of one hundred million citizens within each of those immense towers.

Where as Reymond was the last survivor without genetic modifications, since thanks to recurring organ transplants every half century, he had prolonged his life for more than three hundred years.

Nor could he avoid standing out for his white and gray hair, plus his aging wrinkled countenance, among the new population of human beings with a rather young and almost automaton and moderate appearance. Furthermore, that he did not endeavor to change and adapt his irreverent and generally rebellious behavior towards the norms in force in that new and disciplined world order.

In which his excesses were allowed, by exception only towards him, because he was the last being of the "seed" generation.

As the ancient population that lived before the tragic death, which occurred more than three centuries ago and historically called the death of ninety-three percent of the existing population in those uncivilized days, was historically called. Without anyone having been able then to do anything to avoid the death of those almost six billion inhabitants.

Being Ilana in those modern days, and for living next to Reymond. Who, in addition to directly and tacitly allowing him those various irreverence's and strange habits of another time, had also gotten accustomed little by little, until repeating herself sometimes, those irregular extravagances that he repeated almost daily.

- Why don't you allow Dad, to improve your life with a new cloned body? - She had said many times.

When after reaching her a small cup with medicinal infusions, to alleviate some discomfort in her tired body, she did not avoid noticing the marked wrinkles on her father's equally exhausted face. Which made Reymond look even older because of the striking white hair that he had been wearing for a couple of centuries.

- I do not do it! - He sometimes answered - Because I fear that I would lose all my memories. Although they tell me that I would have them stored in my genetic memory - he added later and with emphasis on that last sentence, before the possible arguments of his daughter, who was speechless and with her mouth almost open, looking at him with affection and a short smile.

Since, among a whole population of millions of people who looked quite young and not older than twenty, Reymond always attracted attention when he left his home, due to his smaller size than the others, and even with a meter and seventy centimeters tall, barely reaching the chest of the others. As above all for its remarkably smiling appearance, quite aged with its wrinkles and gray hair.

That, although it was a very strange characteristic, in a whole population of beings so young and tall, like a fly in a plate with white milk, they also made Reymond an almost famous character for his extraordinary peculiarity.

In that many of those beings with young and pale faces, despite already being around three hundred years old, did not avoid approaching him with expectant eyes, in addition to a certain rational curiosity.

What they might have thought was some kind of fanatic emotion, if they hadn't always kept their faces almost frigid and expressionless, looking him up and down.

But that ended up being something quite normal and even every day for Ilana. That, despite maintaining the similar cold and distant attitude, without affection or physical contact in public and among all the other human beings who lived like her in the mega-colony.

As was the norm of behavior accepted by current society, since the world devastated by death and the epidemic was rebuilt three centuries ago.

She also could not avoid discreetly and in the privacy of her home, letting loose all her hair, after freeing herself from that obligatory high bun hairstyle or that tight ponytail behind the head, which women used almost at all times.

In which Ilana also shed the psychosomatic armor of repressing her emotions and feelings. That, despite having been programmed into the psyche since birth, as it had been with all cloned beings. He did not prevail in her before the continuous hugs, with kisses and affectionate words, that he was receiving daily from Reymond.

That after awakening in Ilana, some of those hidden and guarded vestiges of repressed humanity, it did not take her long to infect them little by little and day after day to her friend Evans.

Who after that unusual mutual contact with the lips, was not the same, until many times surprised with an unexpected smile when thinking about her.

Which was what led Evans, also to take refuge in Ilana's home, to stop pretending the almost automatic attitude that everyone else carried through the corridors and corridors of the intra-city where they lived.

Where it was inevitable that in addition to talking to her, he would have done the same with Reymond. That he kept telling his old stories, naturally and frankly in every word with which he remembered the past.

Each new experience being incredible for Evans, like one of those afternoons. In that, listening to music, he could not deny, with laughter of surprise and expectation, Reymond invitation to dance with Ilana for the first time.

That in addition to taking Evans on an imaginary journey through the clouds, when he turned and turned dancing, while he was holding her hands. It also woke up in his chest, the desire growing stronger to give him another kiss on the lips.

- What have I done? - He said - Excuse me please! - He added later and after he had done it, to leave with a true tone of regret and shame on his face.

While Reymond and Ilana, they just stared at each other and looked at each other, when they saw him say goodbye in a sudden hurry, after half interrupting that dance, to come out with his face down from that house.

- What happened? Reymond asked.

- I do not know! - She replied - But I think we woke up something in Evans' heart!

That ended up being a truth that no one had ever anticipated, when the structures in the chromosome chain were reprogrammed, to also inactivate the neural networks that would preserve genetic memory.

- What is happening to me? - Evans said to himself, every new morning he woke up with that unusual desire to get up smiling.

Without removing from his mind, that sequence of images that he had had in his dreams.

Where he recognized himself with Ilana, with different clothes and slightly changed features. He stood behind her and pushed her back with both hands, to propel her forward in that hilarious rocking she enjoyed sitting on an old swing that hung from a sturdy tree in the backyard of an old house. Of those that were only seen in the historical records of the central database.

And though the memories of those dreams seemed so real because of the smallest details, as if they had already been lived, Evans knew by logical reasoning that this idea was more than difficult, if not impossible.

Because for three centuries, no one had dressed in such a colorful way, not even in cotton and polyester clothes. They had been replaced by white semi-organic tissues, in all their basic biomolecular structure. That, despite being thin and aseptic, as very soft and flexible, they also adapted to the physiological temperature of the bodies they were covering. Increasing the heat in the fabrics when it was cold, in the same way that it happened in reverse in the hot times of summer or spring.

That while it wasn't that aesthetic part or the fashion of the dresses that absorbed Evans's thoughts, he also couldn't ignore a growing obsessive fixation, distracting him from his medical research, thinking every minute of the day about facial appearance. from Ilana.

Who, despite feeling the same tingling and throbbing in his chest, did not stop showing a completely feigned *indifference, being with him in public, and more than anything else among other people.*

That they also began to notice, as both did not comply with the allowed social distance of one meter or more between each individual.

In addition, that Ilana did not avoid confessing one morning after school, that in the same way she had also been having for several months, a similar sequence of those same dreams.

In which dressed in extravagant designs and colorful clothes, the two walked through unknown irregular streets open to the reddish blue sky. Sometimes holding hands or even hugging and close together, to end almost always with a kiss when both say goodbye.

As she, who was first encouraged by trust without repression with Reymond, to ask her father, what did he think about those repeated images that lingered in his mind, even after being awake.

- I think they are memories! - Reymond told her, at that very moment that she had finished narrating the whole dream.

- Memories? - She asked, with inevitable bewilderment on the expression on her face - Whose or when? - He added later, after fixing his eyes and all his thoughts on the possible response of the one he called dad.

- Best regards, my daughter! - His father said, making a brief parenthesis in his comments, before continuing to speak - I think and understand, they are also the

same ones that have awakened in the neural cortex of your friend Evans!

But as much as he wanted to tell her more, and to have revealed every ancient secret that had slept in his old man's heart, Reymond closed his eyes for a moment, giving his daughter a warm kiss on the forehead, as he did when saying good night.

Then repeating with mysterious sweetness in each word he said, that the memories of a past life are sometimes reborn with the love that has been sown in the hearts of souls who are twins.

- Does it mean that I'm in love with a soul mate? - Ilana exclaimed, with evident joy in her voice and in her gaze.

- So, it seems my daughter! - Reymond whispered, before seeing her go with effusive enthusiasm towards her rest room.

Although he was not oblivious to what might have happened in the minds of those two young men, to say the least, and despite the fact that each one was about three hundred years old.

Reymond did not hesitate to stay awake most of the night, rummaging through the memory files, which he himself had encrypted in the central database, more than three centuries ago.

With the luminous idea of discovering, how the blockade inserted in the genetic code could have been deprogrammed for the entire neural network that articulated past memories, in each being cloned in the amniotic chambers.

- This is almost impossible! - Reymond said to himself.

When it was already dawn and when he realized, after comparing the synaptic records of Ilana's cerebral cortex. That she was no longer the same and had changed in the course of those three centuries. Or perhaps with more success in the last ten years.

Because looking at the patterns of the neural structure in Ilana's brain, it was evident that nothing had remained static. Noting he, that in addition to an increase in the number of neurons in his daughter's head, the entire structure of his complex neural brain network had also been reconfigured.

That, for Reymond could be perhaps the answer so that his daughter and perhaps even Evans, had achieved by themselves, the awakening of all the memories preserved in their genetic memories.

That is why that next morning, and with the idea of leaving any doubt, also assuming Reymond, from whom Evans would have been cloned, by the unmistakable name Jacob that he had as his last name.

Without looking very interested, so as not to arouse unnecessary suspicions in his daughter's mind, he as a father, preferred to wait patiently for Evans' next visit.

That, taking longer than usual, he did not show up in all that long month nor in the next, resuming his visits to Ilana's house only after a third month of absence.

- How are you sir! - It had been the greeting of Evans, when entering something crestfallen to the house of Ilana.

- I feel good! - Reymond replied - And how are you, son? - He added later, with a warm tone in his voice, to soften the rigid attitude and especially the evasive look of the boy.

- He is a little puzzled! - Was the comment of Ilana, who was a couple of steps behind her friend, after having closed with a code the tempered glass door at the entrance to the dwelling.

That it was something that father and daughter did discreetly, to avoid being surprised by the small automated security and surveillance drones, which roamed stealthily through all the two hundred levels of the urban mega city, in which they lived together with the other one hundred million citizens. .

- Excuse me sir, if I disturb you with irrational behavior and out of allowed social protocol! - Evans said, after standing and with a very rigid attitude, in front of the affectionate sight of Reymond.

Who, in order not to offend the boy's disciplined conduct, did not rush to break the almost automatic formality that Evans was showing him and was habitual at all times, for the last three hundred years.

- I understand that getting out of the margins can be strange sometimes! - Reymond replied, directing his eyes for a moment towards Ilana's face - But there is nothing to worry about with me! - He added later - As surely my daughter had already warned you!

- It was the same! - She added, with a smile - Although he did not come just to apologize! He concluded then, briefly crossing his gaze with Evans.

Who, nodding his head up and down, exclaimed with a low tone in his voice, who believed that only he, and having lived in that ancient time full of uncontrolled emotions, would be the only person who could help him. To understand the recurrence of strange memories that appeared in his mind, along with those feelings and emotions that surfaced in his chest when he was close to Ilana.

- That's love! - She murmured, with an air of greater wisdom - Which is the same as saying that you are in love!

- It is most likely without any doubt! - Was the calm response that Reymond also gave him.

But, although such words seemed something that was going to break the entire disciplined scheme of life of that technological and quite advanced society, unchanged for more than three centuries.

Evans' reaction was not so extreme, as he sat more relaxed and after hearing, that the same thing had happened with Ilana. As a result of continuous regeneration, he was beginning to transform their bodies in an almost evolutionary way, and had apparently started with modifications to the very structure of his brain.

- So, we can revive this type of memories stored in genetic memory? - Was the thoughtful questioning made by Evans.

- *Effectively! - added Ilana.*

- And it's only the beginning! - added Reymond, thinking within himself, that it would not be the only revelation that he would be forced to tell them in a short time.

Because feeling that he had already lived long enough to see that incipient transformation, that would return humanity to all the six hundred million people, who had cloned themselves to not know death.

Reymond smiled silently, after Ilana's joy, when he announced to his father that they would also celebrate Evans' new birthday in a few days.

- Then I would like to give you something! - Reymond said, fixing his gaze on the boy's face - I wish I could give it to you before entering the medical operating room, where I will receive, like every fifty years, another routine organ transplant to continue living.

- Of course! - Evans replied - It will be a great honor to receive something from you!

Transcending those words of commitment from the environment to their minds, which could be realized in a few days. When Evans visited Reymond, hours before seeing him go to the aforementioned transplant operating room.

CHAPTER FOUR

The return of memories

That new morning, after waking up and slowly opening his eyelids, Evans did not hesitate to touch a finger on the small blue crystal cyber implant, which, like all others, was behind his ear. To download the sequence of images and voices that he had had in that night's dream, to be able to see them again in the afternoon or during dinner, as he used to do every day, after having met to talk to Ilana.

Who with discreet encouragement and very early had also sent Evans over the matrix data network, a holographic message, programmed to activate when he opened his eyelids upon waking.

Evans was surprised with a pleasant feeling in his chest, when in front of his eyes the smiling face of Ilana appeared, wishing him that he had the best birthday of number three hundred and one.

Although unlike previous occasions, he also could not remove from his head some images that he had apparently dreamed and that without being able to understand, he was seeing in his mind, as if they were coming true and repeating throughout the morning, and even after lunch of that day.

Where Evans looked at himself, though still noticing that he was shorter in stature, as he walked in a hurry and holding hands with a woman in a dark dress and a reddish cotton coat over her shoulders. It seemed to him; it was unfailingly Ilana.

Who, without turning her face in that memory or dream, could not speak clearly to her either, as she wore a small white mask over the middle of the face. That had been the thing that most attracted Evans' attention in the dream, noticing how that white cloth filled more with red drops, after each occasion Ilana touched.

- Hold on a little more! - Evans said, with obvious concern in his eyes - We will be home soon! - He added later, with deep regret in each of his words.

- Why don't we go back to the hospital! - she asked, without containing the cough and the shortness of breath. That was accentuated more with that chinstrap covering his nose and mouth.

- Because there is no place where you can be! - He replied, almost with tears in his eyes - All hospitals and clinics are saturated with sick and infected!

- So, what will we do? - She said - If I am also infected with the virus!

- The best thing will be to take care of yourself at home! - had been Evans's answer, in that strange dream - Because I won't stray from your side either! - he finally added.

- Do not leave me alone! - she murmured, unable to say more, from the dry cough and the drops of blood that were gathering in her throat.

- I never would! - He replied, holding the woman's hand tighter, which he assumed was Ilana.

Although waking up from sleep in the middle of that night, not knowing why his eyes were also watering,

Evans could no longer sleep peacefully. Waking up almost every hour, between strong palpitations and a strange feeling of crying in the chest.

That he grew worried and anxious, not knowing the reason or cause of that sinister dream. In that the greatest fear that distressed him was no longer directed at him, but at that woman, who seemed to suffer at his side.

Until it was impossible for him to hide the worry that he had in his mind, after getting up and that was clearly reflected in his somewhat decayed face, that morning.

That Ilana did not stop perceiving from the first moment.

- What's going on? - Was the question she asked him bluntly, seeing repeatedly his gaze lost in the void.

- I do not know! - He replied, after feeling Ilana's fingers holding with affection and softness one of his hands.

Because without being indifferent to the peace and tranquility that she instilled in him, with just the sound of his voice in every word he said. Evans also couldn't help being embarrassed by being next to her. Unable to sort out all her nascent emotions after seeing her smile or sometimes touching her hands.

Which was one of the reasons why he didn't dare to frequently share all his thoughts with her. Although together they downloaded each day and like many, in the matrix network that connected all the people on earth, those images and memories lived daily, or during some dream.

And although neither knew the deception in her actions or thoughts, Evans had learned in recent years with her, to evade or postpone an answer, by changing the order and priority of the concerns in her head.

As he did at that moment uncomfortable in front of Ilana, as he lowered his eyes and spoke the name of Adam Jacob in a low voice.

Knowing that she would recognize the name of her genetic predecessor, and that she had lived at the time of the seed generation as had Reymond.

- Is he the one who worries you? Ilana whispered, turning her face almost in front of Evans's ear.

Who without saying a word just nodded with a slight movement of the head from top to bottom.

- I knew you reopened some memories that apparently were from him! - She said again, referring to Adam Jacob.

- Yes, I did, although they are not very clear and disturb me in a big way, instead of clarifying what happened in those blurred and confused images! - Evans replied - Because in addition the data transfer that I obtained in addition to the matrix network, left me more embarrassed and with a bitter taste in the chest!

- You will say in the stomach! - Ilana argued, with a smile on her face, for having been able to correct her friend, who always seemed to know everything.

- No, because the pain of the truth that I fear, is bitter and it is felt in the heart and not in the stomach - he answered.

- What do you mean? She asked, her calm gaze on his countenance, as she stared at him again.

Still thinking about the next meeting Evans would have with his father.

Because after Reymond's request to see Evans to give him a gift of souvenirs, Ilana did not know whether to add more information, it would not end up stunning her friend's mind more in confusion.

Although not forgetting Evans' words, it would be an honor to receive information from Reymond's mind, when noticing some admiration in him for his dad. She had continued preparing as a previous birthday gift, that Evans would interview her father, even when the old man was on the stretcher and prepared for that routine medical organ transplant, which was done every fifty years.

Where unintentionally and for having gotten so well between the two, the old Reymond did not object to connecting the electronic device behind his ear, in a wireless link with Evans, to transfer most of his memories lived during the catastrophic death that had almost extinct to the world, three hundred years ago.

CHAPTER FIVE

A truth is discovered

Although information on any subject of knowledge was available on the global data matrix network, where anyone could connect with a wireless signal, through the small blue glass device placed in everyone at birth behind the ear.

Something that had caught Evans' attention, but that he did not give much importance at the time, was not having found detailed and specific information about the events related to the great death in the past.

That it had been the fact that changed the course of the world and of humanity completely.

Because although they seemed incomprehensible as strange and absurd, everything made sense again in Evans's head, after that afternoon when he was meeting with Reymond Cox.

By linking his mind with the thoughts of the old Cox, Evans began to live the clear and sequential memories that for years had haunted the life of that last survivor of the seed generation.

- We will make it! - They were the most outstanding starting words in Reymond, that Evans began to extract in sequence of memories, from the same head of the old man.

- Yes, we will make it Dr. Cox! - He could also hear from the mouth of another man, in that same memory.

In that, dressed in the same way, in a long white coat, he made him suppose that he was also another doctor, as Reymond had been.

- With this enzyme Dr. Macena! - Reymond said - We will manage to remove the diseases from the world.

- It is true! - added with a gesture of satisfaction that other doctor named Bruno Macena - Eliminating sick genes will eradicate ill health and prolong life in all newborns.

Whose conversation was not at all confidential, became the news of the moment and soon passed by word of mouth, among all the other investigating doctors on the team in the laboratory.

Coming in the same informal way and quite quickly, to Adam Jacob's ear. That he was then one of the administrative directors of Corporate Laboratories.

- Is it true what I heard? - It had been the question that Adam asked on the phone, when he had called from his office to the phone that Reymond Cox had in his laboratory.

- So is! - Reymond replied - We already found the super enzyme! - Then added, without receiving a response from the other side, more than the dry sound of the phone when it is hung up.

Because without waiting long, they did not take long to see the slim silhouette and dressed in a dark suit of Jacob himself.

- Then you finally did it! - It had been Adam's exclamation, with a smile on his face. At the same time that he extended an arm to the front, to shake the hands of Reymond and Macena, who were in charge of that laboratory.

- It is still incomplete! Cox preferred to answer, with some caution in those words.

- What do you mean? - Jacob asked, with a tone of voice, which suddenly changed from happy to annoyed.

- That the super enzyme will not be complete, until we successfully test it! - added Dr. Macena, to mitigate the obvious annoyance and anger of that young owner of the company.

- Well, you like to play with my mind and get upset! - Adam said again, with a new tone of voice more relaxed, as he directed his words towards Reymond.

Without him having answered anything either, when looking at him as many times, only in silence.

And although Adam was not entirely to Reymond's liking, neither of them could refuse to work together, researching new medications.

At that direct request from Jacob's dad, who had been the benefactor who had paid for years, Reymond's college education.

So, in the face of that debt of honor rather than money, Reymond Cox had promised to work at Corporate Laboratories, which was the main company of the Jacob family.

- This is something that deserves a celebration! - Adam had exclaimed, without avoiding taking Reymond out of his musings, when he uncorked an icy bottle of champagne, which opened in the same glass entrance of that small laboratory.

- But nevertheless, there is still a problem! - said Dr. Cox, when almost all the other doctors were holding the glasses in their hands, and they were also preparing to listen to Jacob's brief speech.

- For now, I don't want to hear anything negative, until I test the enzyme! - Adam had said, with some annoyance, which he tried to hide in his words, and without turning to look at Reymond's almost smiling face.

That, without boasting any premeditated success, he also did not avoid having the same conversation with Macena, the next morning, when they would carefully test the enzyme.

But although the joy of those past thoughts was evident and in Reymond's mind. Evans continued to review the old man's memories, stopping again for another subsequent conversation Cox had had with that same lanky, eclectic Dr. Macena.

- But what will we do with the epidemics? Was the question Reymond was asking his other colleague. Thinking that, throughout history, the virulent epidemics had taken the lives of millions and many times decimated the population of the entire world.

- With just the super enzyme nothing would be totally effective! - Macena had replied - Until the subjects are infected with some anti-virus that immunizes them completely! To make the super enzyme more applicable! - I had finally added.

- So! Would all our work have been in vain? If we don't carry some dead-on top! - Reymond murmured, with some anger and a deep feeling of sadness and emptiness in each of his words.

- In that case! Everything would fall apart, without a previous test that prepares us for the unforeseen! - Macena added again, with ill-fated resignation and not daring to look him in the eye.

- But what do you expect us to do? - Reymond exclaimed again, with obvious annoyance in his eyes - Because I'm not a murderer!

- We would only have to infect a few test subjects first, with potent virulent evil, and then create the antibodies for life!

These being the last words of that memory, which echoed in Evans's mind, as he took a short break in the transfer of memories. Rather than startled and even a little scared, he would start receiving new images and thoughts from Reymond's head again.

In which a feeling of deep anguish could not be avoided either, when through the memories of the old man, Evans first contemplated the images of an old television newscast.

Where the aggressive emergence of a new influenza or influenza virus was reported, which, according to the reporter, had originated in a communist country in North Asia.

Making Evans think for a moment, with a smile on his face, that it was inevitable in that distant time at the beginning of the twenty-first century, that the mass media in the West, self-appointed capitalists, had generally sought to leave governments that they called themselves communists or socialists.

Although, after advancing more in Reymond's memories, Evans ended up erasing the brief smile from his face, when contemplating new news and television fascicles.

Where there was no lack of voices or phrases of alarm and fear, which exclaimed how that epidemic was far from being just a flu or influenza.

In which also, his agile mind and linked to the head of the old man, led Evans to new memories stored among the memories of Reymond.

- How dare you do it? - It was the question that Reymond had asked with demanding anger, while he raised his hands, rebuking Dr. Macena, who was standing in front of him and with his face down.

Reminding old Macena with those harsh words, as a few days ago, Adam Jacob had intercepted him in the hallway, with that look full of intrigue and malice. That sometimes it intimidated him so much, for no apparent reason.

- Dr. Macena! - Jacob had said to him that morning, without stopping to look at the aged appearance of that man who was twice his age in years - What do you plan to do now? when Cox seems to have abandoned him.

- I wouldn't say that! - Macena murmured, with the intention of avoiding a direct response - Dr. Cox is a brilliant and honest doctor. And if he doesn't want to get involved, I wouldn't doubt his intentions!

- So, without someone to run this lab, there would be no choice but to shut down the enzyme project! - Jacob said with some malice.

Knowing that, although Macena did not have the courage or intelligence that was required for the transitional position. Nor would he refuse to take responsibility, lest he see how all his life's work was lost.

- But none of that has to happen! - It had been Macena's argument, with an unusual conviction in his words. Without losing that customary glow of fear in the eyes.

- Being that way! - exclaimed Adam, in a low voice - There would be nothing more to discuss between us! - He added later, as he put a hand in the pocket of his jacket.

From where Jacob extracted without much hesitation, a pair of security keys, which he handed to Macena after extending his arm. Knowing that this man would recognize them as the only keys to the most secure vault in the entire lab.

Where they were stored with protection, each of the samples of those various viruses and strains of contagion.

That, due to their lethal danger, after having been tested on animals, they were never tested on any human being. Just to be stored in that peculiar vault that was in the basement of the laboratory.

- What is this? - Macena murmured, with feigned naivety in that question. At the same time that without saying anything else, he only extended a hand to receive that pair of keys.

- It means Bruno, that everything will be in your charge from now on! - It had been the response of Jacob, without showing any expression of pleasure on his face, and that he did not bother to hide before the eyes of Macena - I hope you keep me informed! - He also added finally, before continuing to walk long, down that wide and silent corridor, towards the elevator that would take him to his office, in the administrative section of that building.

Because without having transcended that conversation beyond that enclosure surrounded by tempered glass doors.

Neither out in the world, any government had been able to contain the epidemic that the two had initiated with the known vaccines.

Nor had the new disease been prevented from spreading from one country to another. Infecting in just a couple of months more than half of the world's population.

That is why it became a pandemic, when it was announced with evident fear in the news.

In which people suffered between symptoms, first fever and redness of the eyes, weakening then little by little, between recurrent coughing attacks. Until after two weeks with increasing difficulty breathing normally, many of them died after fainting or sleeping peacefully.

Being young children and the elderly, those who died first among the pain and crying of their relatives, worrying even more the statistics of contagion and death, which led to the assumption that in just under six months almost all would die, referring to a total of six billion of the total human population on earth.

That was the reason for the governments of the different infected countries to establish strict quarantine measures and border closings to prevent the entry of new infected people.

Arising from the increasing number of deaths, which exceeded the capacity of cemeteries, many cities had no other option than to resort to the cremation of the corpses.

In addition, that, with the collective panic, there was also no shortage of looting and robbery of the food markets. That originated countless other violent confrontations between people and street citizens, against the police and the military.

Although some rulers were not lacking, who, given the appearance of the first outbreaks of the virus, with feverish symptoms and little cough among some populations, preferred to ignore the recommendations and warnings of public health.

Urging in his political speeches, to continue with the daily chores, instead of putting himself in a safe place.

- We cannot stop working, under the threat of a false disease! - exclaimed one of these presidents of government, when he was interviewed by the news programs of that time.

Although it did not take even a couple of weeks for that same subject to publicly declare that he had been wrong and changed his mind, with evident pain on his face.

But as is often the case with late regrets, not even with the daily use of face masks or latex gloves on the hands, there was very little that could be done to avoid the initial death of the infected.

That, unlike other epidemics of influenza or influenza, which was what had been believed at first of the contagious disease due to the similar symptoms, it did not take long for the deaths to be announced in the news, first by hundreds daily, and then to pass at almost thousands an hour, reaching hundreds of thousands in a short week.

Given the incredulity and expectant fear of almost all citizens, in the various countries, regardless of whether they were from the first, second or third world, as they called themselves back then.

- We are facing a pandemic of lethal implications! - Other presidents of governments said, without knowing either what to face the collapse in their hospitals and medical clinics.

Where the first infected patients were treated with fear even by doctors, who likewise fell victim to the same feverish symptoms, until gradually joining, among the countless deaths from the virus. Invisibly, he did not discriminate against anyone.

Because despite the containment mechanisms against the epidemic, and which became general in all cities and countries. Nor did the joint and constant patrol of the military and police, since quarantine states have been established in many places, prevent the transmission and spread of the contagious virus.

Because the deaths of loved ones were not enough, the pandemic nightmare was just beginning.

With repeated scenes of pain and suffering, where thousands and thousands of infected and critically ill patients lay on the floor of corridors and corridors of various hospitals, as there was no space or beds available to adequately care for them.

As it was happening after the deaths, the boxes with dead accumulated in the streets surrounding the saturated cemeteries.

That, due to the urgent emergency, they had no choice but to bury up to three of those funeral boxes in the same grave.

Which also motivated then to incinerate all the bodies of the deceased, due to the stench and bad smell that the deceased began to give off, exposed to the heat of the sun and to the elements, by not achieving a timely burial.

Although, however, everything seemed to change one day, during the third month of the pandemic, when knowing that more than ninety-nine percent of the world population was infected, it was announced by all the mass media, that the long-awaited vaccine had already been created and would be freely available to all interested governments.

That is why between laughter and exalted screams of joy, despite the fact that nobody stopped praying the deceased, who numbered in the hundreds of thousands in the various cities. One by one, all the people received that blue vaccine in their arm, which was announced would save their lives.

While Evans, for his part, continued to observe those scanned thoughts, ending with a short sigh of relief, believing that he had finished all that tragedy relived only in his thoughts.

However, after continuing to review Reymond's memories, Evans did not shy away from letting out a few tears through his closed eyes.

Since, although no one remained without having been vaccinated, the application of the dose did not have the expected effect in ninety percent of all those infected.

Because without knowing that stumbling block, what had gone wrong? The most obvious answer was that the virus had mutated and was no longer the same virus that had originally emerged.

- What happened Dr. Cox? - It had been the question that Macena asked, eyes wide with fear, and that Evans listened again through the memories of old Reymond.

"The virus changes every minute," was Cox's response, after lifting his face from a small electron microscope.

- So now what shall we do? - It was Macena's new questioner.

- The truth is that we could do nothing! - Reymond whispered, with a deep regret in his voice - Although there may still be something to prove! - He added without hiding a certain enthusiasm in the hopeful expression in his eyes.

- What do you mean? - Macena said - What do you have in mind Dr.?

- The only thing that we have left and that we have not yet tested - was Reymond's reply - It would be applying a dose of the super enzyme!

Because with that saving idea, and being Reymond Cox the chief doctor of the Corporate Laboratories, in charge of finding a cure for the dreaded pandemic, at the end of that week, that enzyme was applied as if it were a new booster vaccine, with the secret hope that it would do some good.

Although emerging what no one expected, in the first days after that second vaccine, nothing prevented the patients from continuing to die. In which only nine out of a hundred infected people, worldwide, managed to recover.

But that was only the beginning of the grotesque biological accident, of combining that virus immune to vaccines with the super enzyme.

Because after the deaths continued, strange reports began, that after twenty-four hours the deceased people woke up again like from a dream.

Rising by the thousands at the beginning and then by millions, in the cities and countries of the world, all those living corpses.

That with pale and even putrefying faces, they did not hide the sadness and anguish, for the fear caused among their relatives and loved ones.

In addition, they also could not find a way to end their sad lives, although many tried, either jumping from the bridges or from the highest buildings.

After a couple of months, barely ten percent of the entire population that inhabited each of the cities had become undead.

That with resignation and without missing tears of sadness, they were in charge of collecting and incinerating the smelly and decomposed bodies of those other people. That, without being able to die normally, they were wandering aimlessly and without rest until they fell to the ground with the rigidity of a dead person.

Many of them prefer not even to get up, despite the pain they felt with birds and other creatures of prey, devouring the decomposition of their bodies.

That it was not more oppressive than the emptiness and suffering, that seized their souls trapped in those living corpses.

- That was what he did? - Evans exclaimed, interrupting the transmission of those memories he was sharing from the old man.

- I know! - Reymond replied, lying on the table and with a tired expression - I know and I regret it! - He added later, without opening his eyes - But I was not the only one responsible, and I wanted you to be the one who precisely knew! - He finally added, slowly opening his eyelids and fixing his gaze on the boy's face.

- What do you mean? Evans asked, curious and surprised.

- Because I recognized you from the first time, I saw you with my daughter! - the old man murmured in a low voice.

- Did you recognize me? I do not understand? - were the new questions from Evans, who did not seem to like the tone and direction of those words.

- That's right son! - Reymond said, with a more understanding gesture - Because you are the living image of Adam Jacob!

- So is! - Evans replied - He was my genetic predecessor!

- Then you will understand everything, if you continue reliving my memories! - added the old man, closing his eyes again.

Letting the boy resume the sequence of intertwined thoughts, until he went back a little further and stopped in a short and aggressive discussion, of Dr. Cox with another subject with familiar features.

That even with the youngest countenance Evans recognized that it was Adam Jacob.

- I will not do it! - Reymond refuted in that memory, throwing a file on the desk of Adam Jacob, who was then the president of Corporate Laboratories.

- Too late, because it's already done! - Adam said, with a smile of superiority and malice - The virus was released twelve hours ago! - He ended up adding with that air of intolerable arrogance.

With whose words Evans resumed that mental bond with Reymond. Doubting in his mind, if that vivid memory had come from Reymond's head, or perhaps even from his own genetic memory, that he was bombarded with images so real and disturbing.

- You better know that! - said the old man, before saying goodbye to the boy.

Who left the medical room with a completely pale and decayed face.

CHAPTER SIX

The start of a mortality

Without avoiding Reymond from shedding some tears through his closed eyelids, after watching Evans leave his room in that medical center. In that, laying his head on the pillow, he did not stop remembering the frustrating and initial moments of that distant morning and more than three centuries ago, when by the news and when he was having breakfast, he found out that he had already been released. dangerous virus, secretly created in the facilities of corporate laboratories.

- How could all this happen, without me taking it for granted? - It had been Reymond's initial claim, addressing with an expression of anger towards Dr. Macena - Am I painted or am I no longer the head of the medical laboratory! - He finally added in a more annoying tone, while he slapped a hand on the desk in his office.

- It is because they forbade us to notify you! - Was the almost trembling response of Dr. Macena, at the same time as he tilted his eyes towards the cold white china on the floor - Also, he is no longer in charge of the laboratory! - He said, with the same gloomy and silent attitude. Without revealing to him that it was he who had already assumed that position.

- What does it say? - Cox rebuked, with a harder voice - Why were they forbidden to tell me?

- Because it would be obvious that he wouldn't accept! - Macena replied, with that same fearful and hesitant tone in every word she said, without taking her eyes off the ground.

- It is true! - It was heard that someone else added, at the same time that the half-open door of that office was also opened.

- Mr. Jacob! - Reymond exclaimed, with a lower tone in his voice, without hiding that he was controlling his evident anger - It was you who forbade them to warn me?

- I had to do it! - He said, without showing any remorse - To be able to later test the super enzyme!

- Didn't you think about all the dead among the infected! Reymond asked, staring at Jacob's face.

- It is a necessary cost, to achieve a much greater good! - Was the answer given by that tall, thin man. After walking from the door, to stop in front of the two doctors.

But without being able to do anything, to change what had happened, Reymond only preferred not to return to the laboratory for a whole couple of weeks, while the news continued to announce that the virus was spreading at exponentially geometric speed. Having crossed the borders of that distant Asian country.

Where Jacob himself had told him, with a knowing and unscrupulous smile, that the epidemic had originally implanted itself, with the certainty that they could control it like any testing ground.

In addition, that being so far away, it would never affect them dangerously.

Which was obviously an unforgivable mistake, when the infected began to appear in dozens and dozens of new countries.

Although the worst was not having released that virulent sample among the various animal cages, from that exotic and peculiar Asian market. But, to aggravate the situation, either accidentally or deliberately, that virus changed its initial genetic structure, after coming into contact with some bats locked in various cages that were in that market for other precarious.

Therefore, it became useless to apply the vaccine previously developed in corporate laboratories. Not being the same virus, it had inevitably mutated, becoming more contagious after affecting the first humans.

That was the main reason, for Adam Jacob to call desperately and very urgently, the indignant Dr. Cox along with all his team, to complete the research work that Dr. Macena had not been able to solve during that couple of weeks and he overflowed completely out of his hands, unable to contain the epidemic that did not stop and was claiming thousands and thousands of victims. In addition to the millions of infected people who kept increasing almost daily.

Please, Reymond. We need you to find the vaccine! - It had been the words of Jacob, who with tears in his *eyes, had lost that firm hardness in his words, and which had always characterized him before.*

Because without being indifferent to pain, with the same powerlessness of not being able to do anything, despite all the money he had in his bank accounts, Adam did not stop suffering when he saw his wife, suffering from those constant febrile convulsions, until even spitting drops of dark blood every time she touched. Without avoiding either that their health deteriorated more with the passing of those new days, in which the epidemic did not stop in its advance throughout the world.

- I will do everything I can! - It was the cold response of Cox, who then felt a certain remorse for the dryness of his words. Having also felt a certain insane joy at that punishment that fate had poured on Jacob's arrogant shoulders.

And although Reymond and Macena did not stop working together again for days and nights, leading the team of doctors. Without leaving the testing lab during that insufficient new couple of weeks. They also couldn't find an effective vaccine, as the virus spread uncontrollably, infecting not thousands, but hundreds of millions of people per day.

- Everything we do is useless! Reymond had repeated, with an expression of weariness and fatigue on his face, when he was standing in front of Adam Jacob one morning.

After having crestfallen entered the enormous office of that one, who was the owner of Corporate Laboratories.

- Do not tell me that! - Adam exclaimed, his face sad - There must be something else we can do to prevent Elena from dying! - He had added, almost with the pleading expression of a child.

- I do not know what else to tell you! - Reymond replied, keeping an unspoken silence when he saw Jacob for the first time submerging himself in that quiet cry.

Because believing that Adam had no feelings or affection for someone, Reymond had hated him with growing contempt, after he had authorized himself to release the initial virus in that distant Asian market.

- But there may be another solution! - added from behind Dr. Macena, who was also present at that very private meeting. Cheering up after being silent and without saying a word in the face of Adam's obvious anguish.

- What do you mean? Reymond asked.

- To the genetic super enzyme, which could alter the disease and prolong life! - said Macena.

- Would it be possible? - Jacob asked with some amazement, fixing his gaze with a pleading expression in Reymond's eyes.

Who, without answering with words, only agreed with a slight movement of the head from top to bottom.

- Then what are we waiting for? - exclaimed Adam, with renewed spirit, while with a hand he wiped from his face those tears that he had shed in his despair.

- It has not been tested! - Reymond replied - And it could even be dangerous!

- Silly stuff! - Jacob said, with some anger in his eyes, showing again that haughty tone of voice in each of his words - We can't be cowards now! - He added later, with a gesture of contempt and without turning his face, before asking Dr. Macena to leave the office to rush all his orders.

- What you will do is not right! - Reymond said - It will be complete madness and I hope that later you will not regret it again! - He added, without getting an answer. While he too left the office without hiding his growing anger.

Since hoping to be wrong, Reymond observed from the nightly news on television, especially, as the following days all people were called to go to medical centers, to receive the second dose of the vaccine. Which according to what was said, would be the solution to end the fearsome epidemic.

In the same way that Jacob had thought, while holding the hand of his wife Elena, while Dr. Macena was injecting her with that peculiar enzyme. They made everyone believe that the second dose of the vaccine was being tried.

- Everything will be fine! - Adam said, with a brief smile, and without taking his eyes from Elena's half-asleep eyes.

- Do not let me die! - She murmured, before closing her eyes again to fall asleep, after the effect of the enzyme.

- I won't let you die! - It was the answer that he whispered almost in her ear, as she bent her face to kiss him on the cheek. No matter that maybe she hadn't heard him anymore.

Repenting after that night, of those last words that he had said to him, without imagining what would come next, and that became a curse that would reverberate in his mind, for the rest of his life and until the day of his death.

Because once that dose of vaccine was injected to the last of those infected, it didn't take even twenty-four hours to see how people, who still died, started to get up again, as if waking up from a sinister dream.

- What have we done? - Macena bruised, almost between her teeth and with an obvious fear in her eyes, as soon as she had entered Adam Jacob's office.

Who did not stop looking at him with that same haughty contempt, that he felt when he had him standing in front of his desk. And that he only tolerated when he could not count on the work and support of Reymond.

- What have we done? He tells me - Adam exclaimed with evident anger in his eyes - Is he so incompetent that he does not recognize the result of his mediocre investigation! - He added with total anger, at the same time that he threw a file with several sheets, which ended up hitting Macena's motionless body.

Who, without contradicting him at all, or saying a word, only picked up those medical reports and statistics from the ground, before quietly withdrawing from the presence of Jacob.

And despite the fact that all belated remorse seemed to be completely useless, no one said anything in the Corporate Laboratories, when the afternoon of the following day they found the body of Dr. Bruno Macena, hanging by the neck and with his own tie, from the solid metal lamp in his small office.

Who also did not escape the fearsome consequence that came after having injected the super enzyme. Because after twenty-four hours, he also woke up from death, to start walking among the living.

Frightening everyone in his path, as also happened with himself, when Macena saw herself in a mirror, with a bruised face and without being able to raise her head, after having fractured a cervical vertebra at that fatal moment when she had died hanging.

And like that pain and suffering, of seeing loved ones rise from the dead, it did not evade anyone nor did it distinguish between rich and poor. Nor was he indifferent to the proud gaze of Adam Jacob.

Who, without holding back his tears, as he embraced Elena's inert body after she had died, also did not turn away from his wife, when after a day, he opened his eyes again, without understanding everything that had happened.

Because once the initial confusion was over, after rising as from a deep sleep, like each one of those who woke up from death, Elena did not remember some moments of her immediate past, resenting the presence of various gaps in amnesia in her memory.

But they did not disturb her too much, with the idea that she would have only fainted, after several days with fever and intense headaches, from the influenza she was suffering.

Which had been the explanation that Adam preferred to give him, while hugging her again when she had woken up, to carry her then lifted in his arms, from the bed in his bedroom to the backyard of his house. Where Elena didn't stop smiling after he sat her on an old swing hanging from a huge tree, and when he started rocking her gently.

- Everything will be fine from now on! - Adam repeated in his ear, every time their bodies approached, when that swing turned back in that synchronized swing.

That, although it lasted only a moment not so long, it was not prolonged either and they had to stop as a precaution, before the dizziness and possible fainting of Elena.

Who, despite the obvious tiredness that seemed to have something pale on his face, also did not know why he could not fall asleep and sleep peacefully when closing his eyelids.

- What's wrong with me? - It became the recurring question that she asked during the mornings of the following days, of that first week.

- Do not worry! - Adam replied - This will happen soon! It's just the late effect of all the medications you received!

That he had distorted, although it was partly and somewhat true, but not daring to tell him all the real facts. Also, that Elena did not leave the house to see the real frightening desolation that was in the streets.

Which was one of the causes for Adam to keep her almost deceived, as the weeks of that unusual first month passed.

In that she did not avoid feeling enormous boredom, by staying inside the house and unable to go outside due to the current quarantine. That Elena, if she vaguely remembered, had established herself to contain the initial contagion of a flu or influenza virus.

That, although she did not remember clearly and more with the passing of the days, in which she seemed to forget almost everything with the increase in her mental amnesia gaps. Nor did he worry much at first, as he also realized that each new day began to gradually lose clarity in his sight.

In addition, the rejection of any type of food became noticeable, which as soon as she felt it in her throat, caused her uncontrollable retching and vomiting. That they were not without small amounts of dark, clotted blood.

- Do not worry so much. It is just the temporary effect of strong medications! - It was the evasive answer that Adam used to always give to Elena's questions.

- Sure, you are right! - she murmured, with a slight smile on her increasingly gaunt face.

Although with the advance of a whole second month, Adam no longer knew what else to answer to his wife, when without being able to distinguish more than shadows in front of his face, as he shuffled closer with the almost mortuary rigidity, she did not stop looking for him. he with unusual anguish and despair, keeping both arms extended forward, so as not to trip over the walls or furniture in the house.

That became a daily torture, with the course of the following weeks, in which, without ceasing to cry completely desolate, Elena did not want to let herself be hugged by that husband. That he watched her with his eyes off after having also cried so much with her.

- What's happening to me? - It had been her repeated question - What have you done to me? - She added after a few days, after the bizarre explanation that her husband had tried unsuccessfully.

- Forgive me! - Jacob murmured, that morning he did not lie to him and preferred to be sincere - Forgive me! - He repeated many times, with his face lowered and without having been able to contain the cry of repentance again.

But with the pain in the chest, and as it was happening all over the world with the millions and millions of undead, who did not prevent the decomposition of their bodies.

One sad morning, after almost three months of agony and suffering, Elena could not bear to continue living in that unnatural and sinister way.

Which ended up asking Adam to take that life from him in the way that he saw or was possible. To burn her completely later, if at all he loved her.

- You know I love you! - were the words that Jacob gave him in response.

And he did not stop repeating with tears in his eyes, while he cut Elena's almost putrefied body to pieces, and then he was gradually burning in the kitchen oven that was in his home.

CHAPTER SEVEN

Hope is rebuilt

As the days and nights progressed for several weeks, that dense smoke was not neglected in all the semi-deserted and abandoned cities.

Because it seemed like the darkest mist with a nauseating smell of burned meat, nor did it stop darkening the skies, like the hopes and dreams of the few million people who barely survived in that devastated world.

But despite all that had been suffered and lost in lives and affection, it also seemed that humanity's next step would be to slowly come to an end. Without missing the discordant voices that were barely audible yet retained some hope of remaining alive.

- Although the world is hell, we can be reborn from the ashes! - It was a phrase that appeared defaced first on various walls, until it became a motto in the minds of especially the youngest.

That was announced later with increasing vigor in the streets and then went on to countless meetings that were looking for a light to get ahead and achieve the reconstruction of their lives and their cities. Until gradually becoming the first voice that was repeated day after day, to encourage survivors to leave their homes and try to rebuild the empty and desolate world.

Because there was also no lack of groups of people and some surviving government leader, who were no more than twenty-five years old, after the death of all the adults and the elderly, and a large part of the children under the age of twelve. As it had happened with most women, no matter how old they had been.

That was the reason why the new scenario of the population around the world had been so decimated that there was only one woman for every nine men, among all the few survivors.

Among which were still registered in the short payrolls, the names of Adam Jacob and Reymond Cox.

Those who renouncing the old rivalry that the two had had since they were teenagers, also preferred to overcome together and no longer as enemies, Elena's painful death. That she had been the woman that made them both fall in love, since the three of them met in those difficult classes that were taught in medical school.

Although it was with Jacob, with whom she had decided to marry, during that last year of academic studies. After nothing prolonged courtship that intercalated between classes, to try to live happily for the rest of the time until he died, as was the philosophy of life that she always proclaimed with her smile and the warmth of her gaze. Sometimes naive and innocent, as well as malicious, when she rambled aloud about the prince of her dreams.

Without avoiding either, that after graduating as doctors, their lives ended up taking very different paths from those they had planned and discussed when they met the first years.

Because even though the three of them had been great medical students, it was only Reymond who continued in the profession, but dedicated himself to the investigation of infectious contagious pathologies.

At the same time that Adam and Elena decided not to practice the medical profession, when he was forced to assume the administrative direction of Corporate Laboratories, the main company of his family.

While she had not hesitated to give up the vocation, because of the deep love she felt towards her husband, to become at all times the educated and beautiful couple of luxury and showcase of a rich and powerful man, as Adam was. Elena knew, first of all, that her love was completely reciprocated by her husband, that she had never hidden from him that he loved her above all else.

Demonstrating it to him with such simple details, such as reading poetry to her in bed or pushing her with soft firmness when she sat on the swing of the huge tree, which they had in the backyard of the house. Where he never tired of seeing her smile, between short laughs as he swayed forward and backward as well.

That he became an incentive for her, with the passage of the first years of marriage, when she also did not avoid noticing the growing arrogant and sometimes abusive attitude of that man she loved.

That Adam made it evident on occasions that he was away from home, he was despotic and insensitive to other people, who worked in his company or depended financially on him.

As Elena noticed more than once and sometimes for no reason, especially with Reymond. That having been a good friend in other old moments and after having become one of the best medical researchers of contagious diseases, he also ended up working as head of laboratories in the company of Adam Jacob's father.

- Why did you marry him? - It had been the question, that one day Reymond had whispered to Elena.

- Maybe she was naive and even silly! - She said to him - But, even so, I knew that he loved me!

- And that's why you didn't mind seeing, how he really was a cruel and ruthless being? Reymond had added, in a rather inquisitive tone of voice.

- Of course not! - Was Elena's answer, with evident indignation on her face and her words, before getting up from the chair, to stand up, with the notorious intention of leaving that office where they were both.

- Don't go like this! Please - was the apology that Reymond quickly gave her, thinking within herself, that she was not to blame for anything.

Knowing, moreover, that he was the only culprit if there was any, for not having the guts at the time.

Without being able to continue talking to her, at the sudden entrance of Jacob to that huge office of his.

- They told me you were waiting for me! - were Adam's words, as he approached Elena, to give her a short kiss on the lips.

- Just over time! - She replied, with a smile and as usual when she saw him - Besides, I was not alone nor did I get bored, while I was talking to Reymond, who was also here, waiting just the same to be able to talk to you!

- That's for sure with him! - Jacob murmured, with another smile directed only at her - Because that's part of his job! - He was adding later, with an evident contemptuous tone - But it does not mean that I have time to attend to him right now!

- I can wait! She said, turning her gaze from Adam's eyes to Reymond's resigned gaze, which also did not avoid moving her head sideways.

- Of course not! - Was Reymond's answer - I'm the one who is beside the point, and it doesn't bother me at all to come back later!

- Of course! - Adam added, without turning his eyes and with a certain annoying tone.

While Reymond only left that office, after having said goodbye to Elena, just with a slight movement of the hand.

- Don't put yourself that way! - she murmured, with the sweet voice she had and a warm glow in her eyes, after they were both alone.

- You know I can't stand him coming to you! Adam said.

- But he is also my friend! - she replied.

- I know! I know! - Jacob repeated, returning to give him a kiss on the lips, as a sign of his apology - Excuse me and don't listen to me! - He concluded again, before taking her hand, smiling again next to her, to leave the two of that office and that huge building.

Whose situation and I remember, although it could rekindle a certain rivalry between the two subjects at that time, more than anything else due to some unfounded jealousy on the part of Jacob's insecurity.

Nor did such resentments continue or prevail, after the absurd death of Elena, the woman who both men loved with sincere affection.

Although Reymond never told her that he was still in love, and only kept it as a deep secret in his adolescent heart, in those early distant years of his university studies.

Which was also not possible to hide for long, before Adam's insightful gaze. That, from the initial moments in those continuous first-year medical classes, he did not avoid recognizing that intoxicating shine of love in Reymond's eyes.

And almost in the same way as he had also discovered in his own eyes, looking at himself one morning in front of the mirror.

Because remembering his life during the first years of college, Adam did not know what to say when Elena had confessed to him, that he felt that he was falling in love with a not so handsome but intelligent classmate.

That was the reason why he would not hesitate to put all his efforts, to make her fall in love, knowing that with his previous words Elena was referring to Reymond.

That, while he was the smartest of the three, and that he was quite proven by the high marks he obtained in exams and evaluations, he did not have the apparent security that Adam showed with most of the women and almost at all times.

Since, despite being equally in love with Elena, Reymond only preferred to get further and further away from her, seeing her laugh very lively and always looking happy with the company of Adam Jacob.

Whose love story was growing during those years of study, until reaching the altar of a church, after Adam asked Elena for marriage, and she had accepted with emotion and a smile.

So, after sharing the illusion of meeting and falling in love with the same woman, neither of those two men objected to working together again, after that death, which the entire world had suffered.

- I always knew you loved her! - Jacob murmured in a low voice, raising and turning his face, to fix an instant his gaze on Reymond's decayed face.

He didn't say anything when he heard it either, and as they both walked side by side through the wide corridors of the main Corporate Laboratories building, in those months after the death of the same woman that the two had loved so much.

- I also knew that you knew! - Was Reymond's answer, after a long moment and when he saw Adam's silence, in which he seemed to ponder the words he would say to him.

- But I really loved her! - Jacob said, as if wanting to anticipate any possible reproach.

That it was unnecessary in the face of Reymond's indifferent silence, who did not answer or speak again, until they both entered the large office that, for months, had been Adam Jacob's workplace.

Whose name was on a golden plaque on the door, with the label: CEO of new projects.

- But I only make one thing clear to you! - Started Reymond, as he sat in that armchair that was in front of Jacob's desk - If we go back to work together, as you are asking me, I will not let you use research to harm the world again!

- That was never my intention! Adam replied, in a muffled voice devoid of his usual arrogance.

- You know that doesn't matter now! - exclaimed Reymond - Besides, I'm not the best one to reproach you for something! - He finally added, with his eyes directed to the ground - Because I'm also the same or more guilty, for not having stopped you!

That he turned on the last occasion, that the two of them touched on that rugged subject with such sincerity. Spending from that day on, looking together for some way to reverse or cancel the frightening effects of the super enzyme.

- It just doesn't work! - Jacob exclaimed repeatedly, with some anger, when lifting in the laboratory the failed tests in the test tubes.

- It has to be something that we have before our eyes and that we have not yet seen! - It was the answer that Reymond had in his mind, when he kept thinking about the solution to that problem.

Without any of them resting on that investigation, which had been going on for a couple of months.

Until finally one morning, it was Reymond who shouted "eureka", with joy and plenty of encouragement.

- What happened? - Adam asked - Did you find how to cancel the enzyme or its effects?

- Nothing of that! - Reymond replied, after placing a test tube next to other test tubes, after inviting his medical colleague, to lower his face and look through the lens of his sharp electron microscope.

- What does this mean? - was Jacob's new question, seeing how those cells regenerated themselves, persisting in their dynamic state, both in a healthy and living tissue and in other dead tissue.

- It means Dr. Jacob! - Reymond said, with a smile - That the solution was always to prevent the cells from dying!

- You are talking about immortality! - muttered Adam, without avoiding at the same time thinking about all the money they could charge for a medicine with such characteristics.

Must interrupt his musings and thoughts, at the abrupt words of Reymond.

That without hesitation told him that thinking about immortality would only be consistent, after managing to extend longevity in the infected who had survived.

In addition to warning him that he would only continue research to prolong life in people, if he removed the absurd idea of taking advantage of the new supplemental vaccine to strengthen the enzyme.

- Of course, I never would! - Jacob exclaimed, with a mock smile, when forced to reconsider and replace his ambitious thought, with the new idea, that his wife would have been proud of him, if he ended up helping to heal all the sick people in the world.

But, although the solution was not instantaneous, in the following months that passed. Reymond and Adam, leading their respective medical teams, did not rest until they found the exact complementary dose to the enzyme.

That, directly affecting the human chromosomal chain, it not only eliminated the more than four hundred diseases that were perpetuated in the genetic code from parents to children, but would also achieve the continuous reactivation of the organic component T4, existing throughout the human body and through the Blood flow.

That it would no longer only function actively until people were eighteen years old, as it had been happening since the evolution of the first hominid being.

Rather, it could still function indefinitely, with the task of restoring and replacing damaged or aging cell structures in each of the organs or tissues of the human body.

That it was the reason for an early and initial joy and celebration in all the doctors in the laboratory, unlike Reymond. That with a hidden gleam of concern in his eyes, and despite the feigned smile he was showing on his face, he could not remove from his mind the inevitable sequence of the procedure to make each one of those facts come true.

Since having solved all that difficult genetic equation, it was not long before the news of that expected scientific discovery, was first spread among the formal circles of regional governments, until reaching the ears of the same general council of the united countries.

That it had been the administrative and political way in which the survivors were reorganized in each country and on all continents of the world.

Concentrating the entire global government by levels, after having assembled the new and scarce population of no more than six hundred million, to live together by non-economic strata, but of skills and knowledge, in the six main capitals of the world, and for each inhabited continent.

That from then on, they were reorganized into similar regional governments, as if they were bee colonies, reporting directly to a high general council, which governed the assembly of the united countries.

From where an invitation came that summoned the doctors Cox and Jacob, to present together with the results of that medical investigative work, before the general assembly of the representatives of the new united nations.

That, although it meant an initial honor, for participating in the reconstruction plans of the world. Neither Adam nor Reymond knew or imagined the reaction of those few elected rulers, before the harsh reality of all that investigation that they had concluded.

Therefore, it was Jacob who explained in detail the effects and causes of the complementary dose to the super enzyme. Reymond was the person who clarified the advantages and difficulties, which would mean affecting the genetic code of human beings.

- But it has to be clear! - Reymond had said at the end of his detailed speech - We can only change the chromosome chain and the genetic code, by forming new embryos in medical laboratories.

- It is true! - Added Jacob - All our bodies could no longer be altered successfully!

Creating with those last words, a profound silence in all the people gathered in that assembly of representatives of nations.

- Does that mean that we are all condemned to die? - exclaimed someone from among those hundreds of people gathered at that meeting, who would decide the fate of the world.

- We're already dead! - Jacob answered from his podium - Or we will wish to be, when the years pass and we cannot die naturally, as our grandparents did in the past!

Achieving again an atmosphere of quiet meditation, awakening the sad memories in the minds of the majority, but in all those rulers. About how their loved ones and turned into living dead, asked them between sobs, to take their lives in any way possible, so as not to continue suffering in that ordeal, in which their decomposed bodies fell apart.

- It's true and we all know it! - added someone else from all that crowd of individuals. That with serious countenances they began to stand up, in support of the obvious decision they would take by collective approval.

- That means that we must sacrifice our current lives, in order to preserve the human species in the next generations! - Said in a firm and clear voice, one of the three supreme characters who directed that council of nations.

Once again, a short silence was repeated, which this time was followed by a collective applause, which echoed in the vaulted surroundings of that enormous building.

- Then it will be done that way! - He was the decisive voice of another of those three authoritarian characters and not older than thirty years.

- We will start as soon as possible to collect blood samples from all surviving citizens! - said Jacob, with the visual approval of all those representatives of the council of nations.

- The first and next generation! - added Reymond - They will be the improved and long-lasting clones of each one of us! He concluded later, referring to the taking of blood samples from the six hundred million survivors.

After which and for a couple of years, they did not stop in the laborious effort of collecting blood samples, which accumulated in a huge medical confinement, owned by Adam Jacob. That it ended up being known as the great biological ark, and that it went without saying, was the last hope that would save the world.

That there was no shortage of choice to do what the biosecurity protocol for preservation established, or to obey the unwritten reasons that were dictated in the heart.

That it was the quiet dilemma in Reymond's mind, which, still holding an old blood sample from Elena, and which he had taken for a pregnancy test, before the epidemic had begun. He also did not know for sure, if he had the right to include that peculiar blood test among the hundreds of millions of blood samples, which would be kept with identifying records in the great biological vault for another twenty years.

That in the end he ended up including, after falsifying the registry to attach the blood sample to his, with the name of Ilana Cox.

Alluding in the observations paragraph of the archive document, that this blood sample would be from her daughter, so that she could be born in the first generation of cloned people.

Without anyone noticing, not even Adam Jacob's insight. To become during those hundreds of years the happy secret in the heart of Reymond.

While following the world reconstruction plans, with the use of whatever resources would be available in each of the surviving nations of the world.

In those two decades that followed, there was not a single person who did not work hard and hard, in the construction of the high and wide six staggered towers of two hundred floors, which would house more than one hundred million inhabitants in each one of the towers built.

That being distributed of one by each continental region, in which the world had been divided, it only favored the revival and conservation of the almost extinct flora and fauna existing. After the almost complete demolition of the old decaying cities and towns.

They were transformed into immense reforestation fields and planted food crops. To sustain the incipient human life that was being cultivated in countless amniotic chambers, waiting to be born, and that would replace people, in every way of everyday life.

Because knowing that after another couple of decades or maybe less, the illness or death of each one of those six hundred million survivors would be inevitable.

With the sure probability of becoming undead. None of them showed opposition or pettiness in their acts and faces, when the moment of the programmed death arrived, each one of them barely closed their eyes after entering the incineration chambers naked.

That having been created in each of the six new and huge cities concentrated in those two-hundred-story towers. It was the last nauseating scene, where the sinister chapter of the biological and tragic accident that had given life to dead people was terminated.

- After I leave, will he be able to remember something? - It had been the question of many people, if not the majority, referring to their clones that would come later to replace their lives.

Although they were not saddened by the answer, which would not happen in all of them, despite the fact that they carried within them the genetic memory, with an archive of all the memories lived up to the moment of the blood sampling.

Because without anyone or anything preventing the planned transition. After a few months in which the new cloned human beings were born, they would take the place of their genetic predecessors, already dead and cremated.

Everything seemed to work in this new world, as if nothing bad had ever happened, and more because nobody clearly remembered what had happened.

With the only exception was Reymond Cox, who preferred only to continue living without being cloned, with the help of various organs transplanted into his body every fifty years.

That prolonging his life in a little more than three centuries, even with certain aging, allowed him to see the fresh and creative personality of Elena's cloned being grow.

That he cared as if he were his own daughter, baptizing her with the similar name of Ilana, with her respective last name Cox, alluding at all times that he was her father.

Although with the total satisfaction of having lived long enough for the next three centuries, as well as feeling that heaviness of his tired old body.

After that revealing conversation with Evans, Reymond also did not feel that it was necessary to continue existing in that game, which every fifty years he did to avoid the cold embrace of death.

So, with a smile on his already tired face, and knowing that this time death would soon visit him, he himself deprogrammed in the data center, that habitual medical intervention that he would have, and that he did just a few minutes before starting that organ transplant surgical procedure.

CHAPTER EIGHT

Lights of humanity

After the unforeseen death of old Reymond. That, instead of having undergone the prefixed organ transplant, and which would have prolonged his life for another fifty years, he left no other option than to incinerate his body, to avoid the grotesque end that would occur after his death.

That, although it was a peculiar and not at all customary event, since there were no human diseases or deaths for three hundred years. There were also no displays of regret and sadness on the millions of faces who were waiting, and who coldly observed the ritual of farewell and burial of the ashes of the late Reymond.

In that it was also impossible to ignore for Evans, that small tear of pain, that he saw slipping down Ilana's cheek, standing very upright next to him.

- What's wrong? - Evans asked, without turning his whole face, so as not to arouse suspicions in others, about that unexpected feeling.

- I do not know! - She replied - It was something I could not avoid! - He concluded with a melancholy tone, while raising a hand to wipe his face with a distracted attitude.

Without avoiding later, both walk quickly and head to Ilana's apartment, to share in complete privacy those expressions of sadness.

That in both seemed to squeeze their hearts and souls, with an exaggerated and unknown violence.

- Why does it hurt so much? - Ilana exclaimed, without containing a soft sob on her face.

- It's another kind of feeling! - was Evans' reply, who also couldn't contain the crying in his eyes.

- I do not know what to do now? - she asked herself, with a quiet attitude - I don't know if I want to live feeling pain like this! He muttered then, resting his head on Evans' shoulder.

Seeming to have the same question mark in his head, he didn't say anything additional either, before closing his eyes with a disconsolate gesture.

The two of us were alone in that apartment on the one hundred and twenty-sixth level, in the two-storey mega-tiered tower. Until falling asleep next to each other, from exhaustion and crying so silently.

As they continued to sit on that large sofa in the living room, where they had both talked to Reymond many times.

- What will I do now that he is not with me! - Ilana murmured, as soon as she opened her eyes, after waking up from her long sleepiness.

Without also avoiding involuntary tearing again. But without moving much to avoid waking Evans, who next to him seemed to have a deep sleep.

- You don't have to suffer so much! - He said to her, with a somewhat muffled voice, and almost between dreams, after having inevitably awakened - Remember that your father is not totally dead! - Then added without opening the eyelids. Who said above all because of the idea, that Reymond would continue living in the memory.

With whose words and without knowing it, Evans had managed to erase the initial sadness on Ilana's face, remembering that all the people had biological samples in the ark of life, that existed in the subsoil of each one of the colonies.

Because getting up with an unexpected encouragement, from that sofa on which she was almost reclining, she did not refrain from also kissing Evans on the cheek, adding with a smile that he was a true genius.

- What happened? - He asked - What do you mean? - He added later, with a certain look of bewilderment, as he also drew a smile on his still sleepy face.

- That you were right! - she exclaimed, as she walked towards the crystalline and transparent console, which protruded from the wide wall in front of her. And that was activated at the contact of your fingers, to fill with bright keys and colored lines.

At the same time that a wide holographic screen that appeared before her eyes, began to show her, the three-dimensional images of a chromosomal chain.

- What did you find? Evans asked, from behind and over Elena's shoulder, after he'd gotten up to walk a couple of long steps toward her.

- It is the most recent access record to the central database! - Elena replied - Where I observe the comparative indicators of the blood samples stored in the life chamber. That my father was reviewing several days before his death.

What was the last thing she said at the time, before slipping her gaze quickly over each written line. In the same way that Evans was also doing it, although with greater care.

- Do you realize what that means? - Was the enthusiastic question that Ilana asked, as she turned her face towards the absorbed face of her friend Evans.

- You mean the genetic comparison? - Was the answer in the form of a question, which he began to sketch with some doubt in the precision of his words.

- Not so much that! She said. "But the record reveals that my father's blood sample was never used and 100 percent of the content is available!" - He added later - To be able to carry out the cloning procedure and bring it back to life, in addition to all the biological improvements that we already have!

- That would be great and great! Evans said, without so much emotion in his words, while staring into Ilana's eyes.

- What's going on? - she asked - You do not seem happy to have solved with your idea the problem of his death!

- Of course, I'm glad to be able to bring him to life! - were the opening words of Evans.

Who preferred to fix his eyes on the holographic screen, before continuing with his answer.

Because continuing with a lower tone of voice, he began to gently raise one of his hands, to point his finger at that percentage indication on the screen. Which showed in a box below, that there was no biological relationship between Ilana and that man, whom she had called dad for almost three centuries.

- Yes, I saw that Reymond was not really my father! - She said - But that does not mean that she had not guided me with parental love all her life!

That it was a truth full of emotion and feeling in Ilana's words, although Evans could not fully understand them. Having lived alone and without any family ties, in that his assigned bedroom, since his birth in one of the amniotic chambers.

Where the entire 600 million cloned people had been created, with an apparent age of almost twenty years.

- So, with all this information available! - Evans said - We can only decide when to do it!

- That's right indeed! - She replied, with another new smile on her lips.

Because having all the security codes required in the system, to start the activation of Reymond's cloning process, with that blood sample that was deposited in the life chamber.

The two left her apartment, not even bothering each to take their customary bath, required as a rule for sanitation and hygiene on all levels of the two-story, urban mega tower.

- You don't think they'll stop us? Evans said questioningly, walking quickly and stealthily along her, through that wide white glass corridor, towards the vertical conveyor that was in the central matrix of the gigantic stepped tower.

- Why? - Ilana replied - For not having bathed? - He added later, with a certain tone of mockery and irony, but without daring to outline a smile in public.

Although it did not become a problem in those risky moments either. Since no security and surveillance drone got in the way of that initial path, until they were both close to taking the central elevator, to go down with the greatest tranquility. Which was the attitude that the two tried to fake, being surrounded by other people throughout that journey.

It was Ilana who was paralyzed for a brief moment, seeing a few steps ahead of her, Aurora's always upright silhouette. That as he moved slowly and seemed not to be talking, he only walked beside Spencer's tall, slim figure. His new research partner, for the mutual change of Evans and Ilana.

Where it was Spencer, who first recognized the tone of voice of his former partner. Because, without avoiding turning his face back, he did not stop his steps either as he ended up surprising Ilana and Evans.

That, coming from behind them, they had no choice but to stop dead in their tracks.

- Ilana! - Aurora said, after also turning her face and recognizing her former study partner. That he remained for a moment, with an almost petrified and immobile appearance.

Without understanding Aurora, like Spencer, because Ilana and Evans seemed to be escaping something, with the paler faces as they were usually seen on a daily basis.

In addition to also noticing unusual drops of perspiration, falling on the foreheads of both.

- What happen? Spencer asked, addressing his words to Evans's face, after lowering his eyes a little and also noticing how he was holding Ilana's hand with warm firmness.

And although hundreds of questions arose in Aurora's mind, as it seemed to be happening in Spencer's head as well. None dared to open their mouths, as they distinguished in the distance, the approach of the routine three surveillance probes, which made their usual round each afternoon in that wide corridor, in that urban sector of the tower.

- I can't tell you now! - It had also been Ilana's response, before continuing to walk, more encouraged by that apparent visual approval of that former research partner.

- Thank you! - It was the only thing Evans murmured, with sincere thanks, as he hurried past Spencer and Aurora's side.

Those who seemed to observe them without saying anything and only with some understanding in the looks.

Since without having heard anything else, while they were walking away. Both Evans and Ilana felt, under that final silence between the four, the strange sensation of solidary help in those two cold-looking and rigid people, as they had been before.

Smiling afterwards and first Ilana, with a gleam of satisfaction and success in her eyes, after going down the elevator and arriving next to Evans, to stop them both in front of the main entrance to the underground and huge life chamber. Located in the basement and below the two hundred floors of the staggered mega tower.

Where she did not hesitate at that very moment, in sliding with a finger the holographic screen that was in front of her face, to reopen that enormous armored glass door.

Without showing any doubt or fear when entering later, and very hand in hand with Evans.

Then stop together, in front of an oval console in the shape of a crescent. In which she and he, standing side by side, began to slide their fingers again, repeatedly activating more than one virtual window.

With access to the central database of the system and in all that old computer network, which had not been used since the twenty-first century, when the great tragedy occurred.

Where with a cool serenity, which was so opposite to the gleam of happiness in her eyes, Ilana quickly moved her fingers on a keyboard projected at the bottom of the holographic screen. At the same time, it entered the data and codes necessary to complete the authorization of the biotic clinical procedure, of reassignment of ortho molecular resources and biological material, directed towards the amniotic chamber.

- But tell me! - Evans murmured, with the obvious intention of interrupting the speed and enthusiasm with which she reprogrammed the closest of the amniotic chambers, in that enormous room full of biospheres, filled with biological liquids.

- What thing? - Ilana replied, without turning her face, keeping her gaze fixed on the indicators. But suspending the movement of his nimble hands.

- Although I know by reasoning! - Evans said - That we are doing something right, albeit clandestine, to get Reymond's life back! - He added later, with more rapidity in his words - What does he tell us, that this is what he would have wanted?

- You are right again! - Was her answer, after having reflected on all the possible options for that question.

Because although there was no automatic security drone nearby, there was no greater surveillance system for any error, than the acute surveillance of the conscience of both.

- Now what shall we do? - It was Evans's question, showing with his words that he would approve of any decision she made.

- It has always been a mystery to understand that bond of mother and son that existed in the past! Ilana whispered, with strange melancholy in her voice.

Remembering also, that Reymond had told him more than once, that, if he lived again, he wanted to feel again the happy experiences of when he had been a child.

- So you want to be a mother? Evans asked, with the same uneasiness in his eyes. Without imagining all the memories in Ilana's mind.

- So is! - she answered, before resuming the movement of her fingers on that holographic console.

To achieve after a couple of hours, it was inevitable to hear the loud cry of a human newborn. That rumbled throughout this silent vaulted room, announcing that child his right to live, in a way that no one had done in the last three hundred years.

- It's a little newborn! - Evans exclaimed, holding the little boy in his arms, after having carefully removed him from that amniotic bubble where he had been created.

- He will be our son! - Ilana added, smiling with an unusual joy, after taking off the white jacket she was wearing, to cover the whole naked body of the little boy with those clothes.

- We will have to feed and raise it, until it reaches a mature age! - Evans said, without avoiding reasoning in the consequences of those acts.

- That will make us your parents! - she exclaimed, with her usual joy, while clutching the little body of that newborn against her chest.

And although it seemed totally strange, no one seemed to realize what they had both done. Because not a single surveillance drone showed up all the way back to the elevator and then to her apartment.

That since that day he turned from both and also from the little one.

But as no secret is eternal, after a couple of years of faking a disciplined and silent life. After the tiredness and boredom of living almost cloistered in a closed environment with two bedrooms.

Ilana and Evans decided to risk everything, to go out one afternoon with the little boy, who was already talking when he was two years old.

Without knowing those two impromptu parents, how they would face the possible rejection of all notorious citizens, or even up to compulsory and forced detention, which implied punishment.

If those surveillance drones, programmed to suppress any disorder, found them as a danger to the proper functioning of the new and peaceful world order, to which all had been subjected for three centuries.

Without avoiding to smile afterwards, first Evans and then Ilana, when looking at each other and with some humidity in the eyes. When they saw a dozen armed and dangerous drones pass overhead. That they did not even stop or notice the two of them, after quickly analyzing the peculiar situation of a child walking in the middle of both, and among all those other citizens.

Which happened differently in front of the other hundreds of people. That, when walking rigidly around them, they could not help but stop little by little, to watch with curious and expectant eyes all the funny movements of the little one.

Where, breaking all programmed social distancing protocol, those other people did not know why, but they began to look at each other smiling. Without restraining some of them, also stooping and taking the little boy named Reymond by the hand.

In that, as something extraordinary and refreshing, Evans and Ilana observed, that more and more of those rigid and expressionless faces, they could not contain the interest of turning their eyes downwards either. Maintaining his sight especially on that little human, who walked on that floor and below his knees.

Being equally surprising to both of them, noticing among that crowd, the faces of Aurora and Spencer.

That with concealed gestures, they had not avoided smiling with caution, after also stooping to touch the child's head, and after having fixed their eyes on the relaxed faces of Ilana and Evans.

Those who did not avoid realizing either, when the four approached and with the boy to the center, as

Spencer had touched with some disguise again one of Aurora's hands.

As it was repeated again after saying goodbye, when he took again with some disguise one of her hands. While Aurora didn't resist feeling that touch from Spencer's fingers either, after walking away with him slowly, as they walked together and side by side.

REFERENCE OF THE AUTHOR

H is Bolivian. He was born in Santa Cruz de la Sierra, on November 15, 1971. Being the seventh son of Marcial Villarroel and Gerónima Siles, parents from Cochabamba.

He has been married since 2010 to María José Lora, Spanish with residence in Barcelona and Bolivia. With whom he shares the love of traveling, taking him to know nine countries throughout his life. Although he always returns to Santa Cruz de la Sierra, where he currently lives.

He has written and published since he was twenty years old. Starting his publications in the "Cultural Supplement" of the local newspaper "El Mundo". Then participating collectively from 1996 to 1998, and as a narrator, in the three annual series of the anthological book "DIGESTO".

He completed a degree in Economics at the public university in his hometown and later studied a Master in Banking & Finance at another well-known private university in Bolivia.

He is currently applying for a Doctorate in Research and University Teaching.

Although he has worked in banking institutions and public entities, as well as private ones, he has not left literary production.

However, after a failed business partnership in which he was scammed, after his thirty years. With the sale of his patrimonial assets, he had to face the coverage of most losses and creditors, in his capacity as administrative manager and documentary guarantor. That even led to him being in prison for a period.

Although with this prison event, also came the beginning of a renewed literary creation. That has influenced so that he had written some twenty-six titles, only in the last seven years. That, when translated into more than eight languages, have allowed the publication of more than one hundred and sixty of his books.

Being the first to be published: A brief narrative Review of memories, and the Anthology of Myths and Legends of Bolivia, already published in several languages and available in more than eighteen countries. Four other novels and two new mythological anthologies are pending publication.

THEIR BOOKS:

TALES / STORIES:

Fragments ... of memories (2016)
Wake up to love (2017)
Wake up to desire (2017)
Wake up to pleasure (2017)
An Angel at Home (2018)

MANUALS / GUIDES:

Practical Manual: Credit Risk Analysis (2017)
Basic Guide 1: The Credit Process and Risk Analysis (2017)
Basic Guide 2: Credit Monitoring and Recovery Management (2017)
Basic Guide 3: Credit Planning and Portfolio Management (2017)
Basic Guide 4: Credit Risk Control System (2017)
Self-Help Guide: Overcoming Every Problem (2018)

MYTOLOGICAL ANTHOLOGIES:
Myths and Legends ... in Bolivian literature (2016)
Myths and Legends of the Bolivian Andes (2017)
Myths and Legends of the Bolivian Valleys (2017)
Myths and Legends of the Bolivian Amazon (2017)
The stigma of the gods ... Creation myths (2017)
The President & The Inkarri Myth (2018)

NOVELS:
Anakzashi Chronicles - The City of the Gods (2016)
Tears and dreams of an abandoned city (2016)
Melodies of the Field - Geromel Silohes (2016)
Melodies of the Field - Pedro Silohes (2017)
Melodies of the Field - The Beginning of a Life (2017)
Love stories and sex (2017)
First love stories (2018)

THANKS

This book would not have been possible without the encouragement of a number of people and friends, especially.

My total thanks to each one of them.

As especially to all of you who spend your time reading each of these narrations, thank you for being there.

Because despite the short time to write it, more than one writer friend did not stop encouraging me to complete it and reach readers who are willing to read it without prejudice.

Knowing that the objective of this book is to use the proceeds from the sale, to help several thousands of families without food in Bolivia.